SandCastle

Let's Go!

LET'S GO

BY

AIRPLANE

ANDERS HANSON

Consulting Editor, Diane Craig, M.A./Reading Specialist

ABDO Publishing Company

Published by ABDO Publishing Company, 8000 West 78th Street, Edina, MN 55439.

Copyright © 2008 by Abdo Consulting Group, Inc. International copyrights reserved in all countries. No part of this book may be reproduced in any form without written permission from the publisher. SandCastle™ is a trademark and logo of ABDO Publishing Company.

Printed in the United States.

Editor: Pam Price
Curriculum Coordinator: Nancy Tuminelly
Cover and Interior Design and Production: Mighty Media
Photo Credits: Comstock Complete, iStockphoto, Shutterstock

Library of Congress Cataloging-in-Publication Data

Hanson, Anders, 1980-
  Let's go by airplane / Anders Hanson.
    p. cm. -- (Let's go!)
  ISBN 978-1-59928-893-2
  1. Airplanes--Juvenile literature. 2. Air travel--Juvenile literature. I. Title.

TL547.H1546 2008
629.133'34--dc22

                                                    2007006655

SandCastle™ Level: Transitional

SandCastle™ books are created by a team of professional educators, reading specialists, and content developers around five essential components—phonemic awareness, phonics, vocabulary, text comprehension, and fluency—to assist young readers as they develop reading skills and increase their general knowledge. All books are written, reviewed, and leveled for guided reading, early intervention reading, and Accelerated Reader® programs for use in shared, guided, and independent reading and writing activities to support a balanced approach to literacy instruction. The SandCastle™ series has four levels that correspond to early literacy development. The levels are provided to help teachers and parents select appropriate books for young readers.

Emerging Readers
(no flags)

Beginning Readers
(1 flag)

Transitional Readers
(2 flags)

Fluent Readers
(3 flags)

SandCastle™ would like to hear from you. Please send us your comments or questions.

sandcastle@abdopublishing.com

Airplanes fly!
They carry
people and
cargo through
the air.

Jet airplanes are powered by turbine engines.

The shape
of the wings
creates lift.

Landing gear is used only during takeoff and landing.

The pilot controls the plane from the cockpit.

Tim helps his father plot their course before takeoff.

14

Someday Jason wants to pilot a glider. Gliders are unpowered airplanes.

Suzy loves to look out the window when she flies.

Steve's family takes an airplane to visit his grandparents.

HAVE YOU EVER FLOWN?

WHERE DID YOU GO?

TURTLE CREEK ELEMENTARY IMC
1235 CREEK RD.
DELAVAN, WI 53115

TYPES OF PLANES

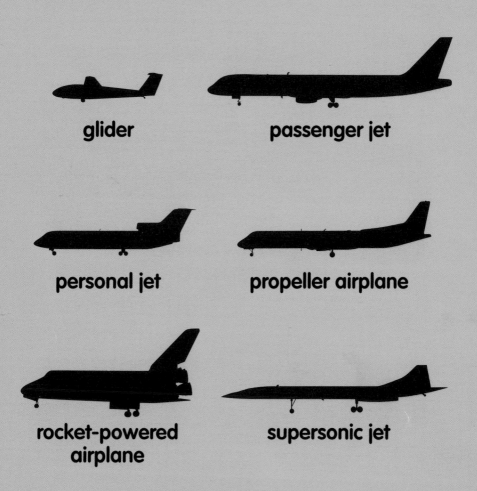

glider

passenger jet

personal jet

propeller airplane

rocket-powered
airplane

supersonic jet

FAST FACTS

In 1903, the Wright brothers were the first to fly in a powered airplane.

The Antonov An-225 is the world's largest and heaviest airplane. It is 276 feet long and weighs more than a million pounds.

Howard Hughes' famous airplane, the *Spruce Goose*, was made of birch wood, not spruce.

GLOSSARY

cargo – goods carried on a ship, plane, or other vehicle.

landing gear – equipment that supports an airplane when it is not in flight.

propeller – a device with blades used to move a vehicle such as an airplane or a boat.

supersonic – faster than the speed of sound.

turbine – a machine that produces power when it is rotated at high speeds.

To see a complete list of SandCastle™ books and other nonfiction titles from ABDO Publishing Company, visit **www.abdopublishing.com**.

8000 West 78th Street, Edina, MN 55439 • 800-800-1312 • 952-831-1632 fax